Phantom
of the
Haunted
Church

Bethany House Books by

Bill Myers

Journeys to Fayrah

The Portal
The Experiment
The Whirlwind
The Tablet

Bloodhounds, Inc.

The Ghost of KRZY
The Mystery of the Invisible Knight
Phantom of the Haunted Church

Nonfiction

Hot Topics, Tough Questions

9803

3

BloodHounds, INC.

Phantom of the Haunted Church

Bill Myers

BETHANY HOUSE PUBLISHERS
MINNEAPOLIS, MINNESOTA 55438

Phantom of the Haunted Church
Copyright © 1998
Bill Myers

Cover illustration by Joe Nordstrom
Cover design by Peter Glöege

Published by Bethany House Publishers
A Ministry of Bethany Fellowship International
11300 Hampshire Avenue South
Minneapolis, Minnesota 55438

Printed in the United States of America by
Bethany Press International, Minneapolis, Minnesota 55438

Library of Congress Cataloging-in-Publication Data

Myers, Bill.
    Phantom of the haunted church / by Bill Myers.
        p. m . —(Bloodhounds, Inc. ; 3)
    Summary: Sean and Melissa continue their sibling banter even as they are
caught up in a dangerous search for a treasure hidden somewhere in the old,
supposedly haunted, church that the town is planning to auction.
    ISBN 1–55661–892–1 (pbk.)
    [1. Brothers and sisters—Fiction. 2. Greed—Fiction. 3. Christian life—
Fiction. 4. Mystery and detective stories.] I. Title. II. Series: Myers, Bill,
1953–   Bloodhounds, Inc. ; 3.
PZ7.M9822Ph   1998
[Fic]—dc21   97–45451
                                                                                   CIP
                                                                                    AC

To Mom:

For putting up with me . . .
and teaching me good stuff along the way.

BILL MYERS is a youth worker and creative writer and film director who co-created the "McGee and Me!" book and video series and whose work has received over forty national and international awards. His many youth books include THE INCREDIBLE WORLDS OF WALLY MCDOOGLE, JOURNEYS TO FAYRAH, as well as his teen books, *Hot Topics, Tough Questions* and *Forbidden Doors*. He also writes and acts for Focus on the Family's *Odyssey* radio series.

Contents

"Watch out! Be on your guard against all kinds of greed; a man's life does not consist in the abundance of his possessions."

LUKE 12:15, NIV

1

The Case Begins

THURSDAY, 16:15 PDST

"If you ask me," Melissa Hunter said, "the whole idea of auctioning off this church is stupid." She stared up at the tall steeple looming over their heads. "I know it's kinda spooky and everything, but it's been a part of our town forever."

She glanced over to the steps of the old, deserted building. A crowd had gathered around, waiting for the mayor to finish another one of his boring speeches so the auction could begin.

Sean, her older brother, nodded. "That's why Dad wants us to cover the story for the station. He figures it will interest some of the local listeners."

Melissa turned to him. At the moment, he was

helping Herbie, the radio station's engineer, plug in a bunch of cables and electronic thingamabobs into the backs of amplifiers and even more confusing thingamajiggers.

As Herbie worked, the accident-prone engineer was talking to their dad over the cellular phone. "Okay, Mr. Hunter, the remote is all set up. We're ready to go on the air. . . . What's that? Oh . . ." He gave a nervous chuckle. "You might have a point. I'll look into that."

"Problem?" Sean asked.

Herbie shrugged as he hung up the phone. "Your dad thinks we might need a microphone."

Sean and Melissa exchanged looks. Herbie was a nice enough guy but clueless when it came to doing anything right.

"Any idea where you packed it?" Melissa asked.

"No, I, uh . . ." Herbie bent down and started rummaging through the piles of wires and cables. "I'm sure it's here somewhere."

As Herbie continued his search and rescue for the microphone, Sean turned back to his sister. "Okay, Misty, I'll go on the air first. I'll introduce the setting, and then if you have anything to add—"

"Wait a minute. Why do *you* get to go on first?"

10

"Because I'm the oldest. Besides, I'm wearing my killer shirt."

Of course, he was referring to the brightly colored Hawaiian shirt,

. . . the one he'd borrowed from Misty's closet a month ago,

. . . the one he'd kept forgetting to return,

. . . the one he now figured belonged to him.

"Sean," Melissa sighed, "that's not your shirt, and besides . . ."

"Besides what?" he demanded as he straightened his collar and fixed his hair for the twentieth time.

Melissa rolled her eyes. What her brother lacked in intelligence, he more than made up for in vanity. "It's radio, Sean. No one can see what you look like on radio."

Suddenly he stopped. "Oh yeah . . ."

"Hello, you two."

Melissa and Sean turned to see Spalding Nathaniel Hathaway III approach.

Neither brother nor sister particularly cared for Spalding. Not because he was rich (although he was the only one they knew who wore designer shoelaces), or because he was spoiled (he was also the only one they

11

knew who had a special butler just to tie those shoelaces). They disliked the kid because he could out snob even the snobbiest of snobs.

Spalding arrived, straightening his bow tie. "Of course, you two will be interviewing my father." It was supposed to be a question, but as usual, it came out more as a command. (With his money, Spalding hadn't much experience at asking for anything.)

"Why do we want to interview your dad?" Sean asked.

"Because Father will soon be the owner of this spooky old edifice."

"How can you be so sure?" Melissa said.

"Because, my dear brainless child, no one has the kind of money Father has."

As usual, Melissa felt her dislike for Spalding rising (right now it was somewhere around wanting to punch his lights out). But also as usual, she forced herself to stay pleasant. "Why does he want this old church, anyway?" she asked. "Because of its historical value?"

"Hardly . . ." Spalding gave a condescending chuckle (which was the only type of chuckle he knew how to give). "Father will be tearing it down so he can proceed to build a parking lot for his new bank."

"Tear it down?" Melissa couldn't stop her voice from rising in concern.

"Certainly."

"But . . . but . . . but . . ."

While Melissa was busy doing her motorboat imitation, Sean stepped in. "If he tears down this church, we'll never know its mystery."

"Mystery?"

"You know . . . about it being haunted and all."

"Certainly you don't believe such rumors," Spalding scorned.

"Well, something's going on there," Sean insisted. "Everyone knows about those weird wailing sounds coming from inside."

"Father says they are simply—"

"And what about those folks who say they've seen strange flickerings up in the belfry?"

"It is simply the reflection from some unknown—"

"And what about the buried treasure?" Sean asked

Suddenly Spalding stopped. "Treasure? Did you say treasure?"

Melissa turned to her brother. This was the first she'd heard of any treasure.

"Well, sure . . ." Sean stalled. "Didn't you know that?

Shoot, everybody knows that." He turned to his sister. "Isn't that right, Misty?"

Melissa simply stared at him. It was obvious she had never heard of such a thing. It was equally as obvious that Sean hadn't, either. His imagination was definitely going into some big-time overtime.

TRANSLATION:
"Big Brother Was Telling Another Whopper."

But Spalding didn't notice. The kid was too focused on the word "treasure" to notice anything. Probably because treasure sounded a lot like riches . . . which sounded a lot like money . . . which seemed to be about the only thing Spalding ever thought of.

"How'd you know about the treasure?" Spalding asked.

Now it was Sean's turn to be surprised. "Well, I, er . . . there really is such a thing?" he asked.

Spalding lowered his voice. "No one is supposed to know."

"Know what?"

"About the pirate's treasure hidden inside the walls."

Sean's eyes widened. "Pirates? You mean pirates actually hid their treasure inside th—"

"LOOK OUT!" Herbie shouted.

All three spun around to see Slobs, the Hunters' wonder dog, heading straight for them.

K-BAM!

Well, she *had* been heading straight for them. Now she was tromping over the top of them, howling and drooling along the way. (Being a bloodhound, Slobs had this thing about howling and drooling—she liked to . . . alot.)

Not far behind, Herbie was racing toward them, shouting, "Come on, Slobs, give it back! Come on, now!"

"Herbie," Melissa cried as she struggled to her feet. "What are you—"

K-BAM!

Now it was Herbie running over them. "Come on, Slobs, bring it here. . . . Come on, girl!"

When Melissa rose (a little more cautiously this time), she turned around and saw Slobs heading straight for the crowd . . . with Herbie right behind. The reason for the little chase was obvious. Between Slobs' teeth was a silvery metal object with a long black cord trailing behind it. A silvery metal object that most life forms

15

would mistake for a microphone . . . unless of course they were a certain dog that had mistaken it for a toy bone.

People screamed and leaped out of the way as Slobs and Herbie raced through them (or in the case of the slower leapers, on top of them). Unfortunately, Mrs. Potts, the Hunters' neighbor (and perpetual victim), was one of the slower leapers.

"AUGHHHHH!"
K-BAM!

And once again she was practicing her famous crash-and-burn routine.

Slobs continued running through the crowd, barking and baying, enjoying her little game, as Herbie continued chasing after her and shouting, "Come on, girl, come on!"

Unfortunately, the little game got a little more complicated when Slobs thought it would be great fun to race up the hill where they'd parked the station's van.

"Slobs!"

Once there, she leaped into its open door, dashed across the front seat, and jumped out the other side.

Unfortunately, the microphone didn't.

Somehow loops in the cable had wrapped around the emergency brake and gear shift. Even that wouldn't have been so bad if Herbie hadn't hopped inside the van to try to help. (As we've already mentioned, ole Herb won't be winning any gold medals in coordination.) Once inside, he tried his best to untangle the cable but only managed to release the emergency brake and shove the gear shift out of Park.

The van started forward.

"Herbie," Sean yelled, "you're moving! The van's rolling!"

No problem. All Herbie had to do was reset the brake and move the gear back into Park. And he would have, except he was too busy getting himself tangled up in the cable . . . first one leg, then the other, then both arms, until he had completely hog-tied himself, unable to move a muscle.

Meanwhile the van continued down the hill, faster and faster, straight for the crowd that was reassembling to listen to the mayor. Well, they *had* been reassembling.

"Look out!" Melissa shouted. "Look out!"

The crowd looked up. The van rushed toward them with the tied-up Herbie staring helplessly out of the windshield.

Once again they scattered, leaping aside as the van bounced past.

Well, almost everyone leaped. It seems poor Mrs. Potts, who had finally managed to get back to her feet, was smack dab in the van's path. She looked over her shoulder, saw the oncoming van, and did what she did best—screamed her head off and ran for her life.

But no matter which way she ran, the van seemed to follow. First to the left . . . then to the right . . . then to the left . . . then to the—well, you get the idea. By now everyone else had stopped and was staring at the performance in stunned astonishment. Until—

"Mrs. Potts!" Sean yelled. "The fire hydrant! Look out for the fire—"

Somehow Mrs. Potts managed to sidestep it.

Herbie and the van did not.

K-RASH!
WHOOOOOSHHHH . . .
pitter-patter, pitter-patter, pitter-patter.

Now everything came to a stop. Well, everything but the water that was now *whooshing* twenty feet into the air and *pittering-pattering* all over the crowd, the mayor, Mrs. Potts, and the van.

18

Fortunately, the collision had loosened Herbie's hands just enough. He reached out to the dashboard, hit the windshield wipers, and numbly watched as the blades sloshed back and forth, back and forth, back and forth.

That about ended the radio coverage of the auction. Come to think of it, it didn't do much for the auction, either. Everyone decided to postpone it until tomorrow afternoon.

But it didn't end the mystery of the church. As water continued raining down, soaking Melissa to the skin, she glanced over at her brother. He was already looking back up at the building, and she already knew what he was thinking. After all, it was one thing to listen to rumors about mysterious wailings and flickering lights. They'd heard those rumors all of their lives. And like every kid with half a brain, they'd gone out of their way to avoid passing the church and its cemetery when it was late at night.

But if there really was a hidden pirate's treasure in there . . .

As Melissa watched her brother think, she had a sinking suspicion in the pit of her stomach—that another case was about to begin for the Bloodhounds, Inc. Detective Agency. . . .

2

A Little Visit

It was later that evening when Sean, Melissa, and Slobs dropped by Doc and Jeremiah's. As usual, Doc was working on another one of her crazy inventions. This time it was a pair of Virtual Reality X-Ray Goggles.

"Just slip them on," little Jeremiah called from inside his computer screen. "I guarantee you'll be able to see through solid objects in the blink of a heartbeat."

Melissa had to smile. Jeremiah was one of Doc's earlier inventions. As a computer-generated character, he had the ability to roam around any computer and pop up on any TV or monitor. That was the good news. Unfortunately, there was some bad. When he'd first been created, he'd zoomed through a phone line, popped into

21

a Chinese fortune cookie factory computer, and overloaded his circuits with too many proverbs and sayings. Ever since then his memory chips had been slightly fried.

"You mean, 'In the blink of an eye,'" Melissa corrected.

Jeremiah nodded. "You hit the nail right on the thumb."

Melissa shook her head in amusement.

"Hey," Sean said as he picked up the X-ray goggles and prepared to slip them on. "Wouldn't these be cool to use at the church?"

"Sean," Melissa sighed, "you're not going to start in on that again."

"I'm telling you," Sean said, "it's the perfect case for Bloodhounds, Inc. Just imagine what we could do with all that treasure. . . ."

"You mean the treasure that you made up," Melissa corrected.

Sean wasn't fazed. "I might've made it up, but Spalding didn't. You saw the way his face lit up—you heard what he said about a treasure being hidden inside the walls."

Melissa bit her lip. She hated to admit it, but he had a point.

"There's something inside that church," Sean continued. "You and I both know it. Something very valuable. And if we can find it before his dad tears the place down—"

"I don't want to even go *near* that church," Melissa interrupted. "It gives me the creeps."

"Come on, you don't really believe it's haunted."

"I don't know what it is, but I don't intend to go inside and find out."

"That's just it," Sean insisted. "You don't have to." He slipped on the X-ray goggles and adjusted them. "Not with these babies. We'll just stand outside the church, put these on, and—" He turned toward Melissa and suddenly stopped. "Whoa, Misty, nice underwear."

"Sean!" Melissa jumped behind one of the counters. "Stop that!"

Sean laughed.

"He's just pulling your nose," Jeremiah giggled from a nearby screen. "The goggles aren't turned on yet. Besides, they're designed to see through walls not clothing."

Melissa nodded but decided to stay behind the counter just in case.

Sean looked over to Doc and signed to her that he was ready. Doc was born deaf, and both Sean and Melissa had been learning to communicate with her through sign language. By the looks of things, Slobs had also picked up a few words because as soon as the dog saw Sean signaling to Doc, she let out a howl and ran to hide under one of the lab counters. The poor animal had obviously seen one too many of Doc's experiments.

Meanwhile, Doc reached over to the small control pack attached to the goggles.

"Here we go," Jeremiah cried. "Let's keep our eyes crossed."

Before Melissa could correct him, Doc fired up the goggles.

There was the usual loud, electronic hum (with a few sparks and flashes thrown in for good measure) until the goggles were finally up and running.

"Are you seeing anything?" Jeremiah asked.

Sean shook his head. "No, not a—WOAHHHH!"

"What is it?" Melissa cried. "What do you see?"

"There's a giant semi-truck bearing down on us!"

"There's no semi-truck," Melissa argued.

"Maybe not here," little Jeremiah's voice crackled, "but there are plenty over on Interstate 5."

24

"But the freeway is a mile away," Melissa said.

"I don't care where it is," Sean shouted, "but that baby's coming right for us. Look out! *Look out!*"

Melissa quickly signed to Doc to turn down the power. Unfortunately, her signing abilities were still a little rough. Instead of asking Doc to turn down the power, she'd asked her to turn it up . . . either that or to order a Big Mac with an extra side of fries.

Doc nodded and cranked up the goggles' power (which of course meant an even louder hum with even more sparks and special effects).

"AUGHHHH . . ." Sean yelled.

"Now what do you see?" Melissa cried.

"It's the Space Shuttle—and it's coming right at me?"

Melissa threw Jeremiah a look.

The little guy shrugged. "Guess they're a bit too powerful."

"Turn them down!" Sean yelled. "Turn them down!"

Once again Melissa signed to Doc, thinking she was telling her to turn down the power (or to add a large Coke to the Big Mac order).

And once again Doc cranked up the power . . . which increased the electrical hum and the light and—

"Duck!" Sean shouted. He dodged his head to the left and to the right.

"What?" Melissa shouted.

"The asteroids! They're everywhere! Look out!"

"We've got him in the asteroid belt!" Jeremiah shouted. "That's out past Mars. Cut power! Cut power!"

"*LOOK OUT!*" Sean shouted, bobbing and weaving. "There's a huge one, dead ahead. It's coming straight for—"

That's just about the time the power pack blew.

The good news was Sean no longer saw a thing.

The bad news was no one else could see, either. Not only had the power pack blown, but it had managed to fill the entire lab with smoke..

Once again Doc's invention had worked in a way that was better than she'd expected . . . but as usual, not in a way she'd intended.

"Sean," Melissa called as she peddled her bike harder to catch up. "Sean, where are you going? This isn't the way home. *Sean?*"

Sean knew he should answer her, but he also knew if

he did, Melissa wouldn't follow. And right now he wanted as much company as possible. Especially where he was going . . . especially at this time of night.

"*Sean!*" At last Melissa pulled beside him and Slobs. "Where are you going?"

They took one last corner and finally slowed to a stop. Fortunately, she had her answer. Unfortunately, it wasn't one she wanted.

"The church?!" she cried. "You took us to the backside of the church?!"

"Yeah." He gave a sheepish grin. "I thought we should check it out one last time. You know, before we go in and explore it tomorrow."

"Explore it? You're out of your mind!"

"What about the treasure and all that money? What about the mystery? What—"

"What about living?" Melissa interrupted.

"Come on," Sean scorned. "It's just some old church. Besides, you know what Dad says about there being no such thing as ghosts."

"I also know what he says about trespassing and being out too late and sticking our noses where they don't belong and—"

"All right, all right, I get the point," Sean interrupted.

27

"But just think what we could buy with all that—"

WOOOOooooooo . . .

He stopped. An eerie wail came from deep inside the church. It lasted only a second before it was gone. Sean wondered if his ears were playing tricks on him. He threw a glance at Slobs. The fur on her neck stood straight up. He looked to Melissa. Her eyes were as big as saucers. So much for ears playing tricks.

Sean swallowed.

Melissa swallowed.

Slobs swallowed.

And then the sound returned. This time louder . . . and longer:

WOOOOOOOOooooooooooooooooo . . .

"Let's get out of here," Melissa whispered.

Taking her cue, Slobs turned and started to run.

"Slobs," Sean whispered. "Slobs, come back!"

But Slobs was in no mood to stick around. She continued racing for home as fast as her legs could carry her.

"She obviously knows something we don't," Melissa whispered.

Sean was just about to answer when something caught his attention. A light. A flickering. It was inside, moving across one of the stained-glass windows.

"Misty . . ." he whispered.

She followed his gaze.

WOOOOOOOOooooooooooooooooo . . .

"Let's get out of here," she repeated.

Sean said nothing.

"Sean, let's go!"

But her brother had other things on his mind. Without a word, he lowered his bike and crouched low. The he darted for the bushes beside the back steps.

"Sean? Sean, are you crazy?!"

But Sean wasn't crazy. Curious? Yes. Scared? You bet. But there was something stronger driving him— something more powerful than his fear or his curiosity. It was . . . the treasure. The thought of all that money. Actually, it was the thought of what he could buy with all that money.

"Sean . . . *Sean* . . ."

He really wasn't worried about going inside alone. He knew his sister would follow. She'd hate it, of course. But not as much as she'd hate standing outside all by herself in the dark. He waited the usual 3.2 seconds and, sure enough, just like clockwork, Melissa dropped her bike and raced to join him.

He smiled. Little sisters—they could be so easy to manipulate.

When she arrived, she gave him a powerful slug in the shoulder.

"Ow!"

Little sisters— they could be so painful when you rile them.

WO*ooo* . . .

"The howling," she whispered, "it's getting fainter."

Sean craned his neck to look around the side of the building. "And the light. It's moving off."

"Good," Melissa sighed in relief.

"Not good," Sean said. "Whatever it is, it's getting away. Come on!" He scrambled out of the bushes and raced up the back steps.

Of course, Melissa gave the required, "Sean . . . Sean . . . no way am I going up there." And of course, in 3.2 seconds she was by his side.

Cautiously, they eased toward the back door. The very door that the faint wailings were coming from. The very door that Sean now pushed against.

"Sean . . ."

The very door that he secretly hoped was locked.

Creeeeaaak . . .

The very door that wasn't.

"Sean . . ." Melissa whispered for the hundredth time. And for the hundredth time, he ignored her. He pushed open the door a little wider. It creaked a little more loudly. There was nothing inside, nothing but deep black darkness.

WOooo . . .

And wailing.

They both gulped. Then Sean saw the light again. Way in the distance. Only this time it was reflecting against a wall.

He motioned for Melissa to follow. "C'mon."

"No way," she whispered defiantly. "I'm not going in there."

He glanced at her. The look in her eyes said she meant business. And deep inside he knew she was right. But he also knew that he couldn't back down. Not now. It was in the *Official Big Brother's Handbook*:

Never Let Little Sisters Think They're Right . . .
Even When They Are

Besides, there was that treasure. . . .

Sean took a deep breath to steady himself. He paused a moment to say a silent prayer, and then he stepped into the darkness.

WOOOooooooo . . .

Was it his imagination or had the wailing grown louder?

He took another step.

WOOOOOOOoooooooooooooooo . . .

The only way he could keep going was to think about the money. Who knows, maybe Melissa could get him a real nice hospital room with it.

He took another step.

WOOOOOOOooooooooooooooooooooooooooo . . .

Or a real nice coffin.

He continued toward the light, inching his way through the darkness. It was important that he not hurry, that he make no sound. All he had to do was sneak up on it, ever so quietly, ever so silently, and—

K-RASH! K-RASH!
BANG, BANG
RATTLE, RATTLE

"*SEAN!*" Melissa screamed.

Normally Sean would have answered, but at that particular moment he was too busy fighting for his life.

First, there was the giant metal monster that had leaped under his feet, trying to make him fall. (Most people would think it was a mop bucket, but Sean's thinker hadn't thought that far.)

Next, the creature tried to make him slip and fall by spewing out its toxic waste across the floor. (Most people would realize it was soap and water from the bucket, but Sean's realizer hadn't realized that far.)

And finally, there was the giant sticklike ghost with its stringy hair dripping deadly venom. (Hey, no one ever accused Sean of lacking imagination.) The creature threw him to the floor with even more *K-RASHING,* *BANGING,* and *RATTLING.*

For the briefest moment, Sean thought he was a gonner. But after rolling back and forth for several seconds (not to mention forth and back for several more), he finally got on top of the thing and wrapped his hands around its thin wooden neck in a deadly choke hold.

He would have killed that monster, too, if the lights hadn't suddenly blazed on and he saw that he was holding a mop . . . the one that he'd pulled from the knocked-over bucket . . . that had spilled its watery suds all across the floor.

That was good news. Unfortunately, there was some bad. . . .

"Misty," he whispered harshly as he scrambled to his feet, "turn off that light!"

"I-I . . . didn't turn it on," she stuttered.

"Well, if you didn't turn it on, who did?"

"I deed," a craggy voice cackled from behind him.

Sean spun around. He wanted to scream and gasp and leap out of his skin, all at the same time. But it's hard doing any of those things when you're paralyzed with fear. . . .

3

Warnings

THURSDAY, 20:52 PDST

A ragged old man with a glowing kerosene lamp stood in the doorway. He leered at them and chuckled. "Zo, you vant zee treazure, too, do you, matey?" His accent was so thick you could have cut it with a knife . . . or a pirate's sword.

Sean continued to stare, his mouth hanging open.

Melissa wanted to answer, but she was too busy imitating her brother.

The grizzly old man broke into a near-toothless grin. "Vell, zee more zee merrier, zat's vat I alvayz zay. Yez zer, zee more zee merrier." He threw in another cackle (just in case there was any portion of Melissa's skin *not* covered in goose bumps). Then he turned and hobbled back into the church, motioning for them to follow.

The last thing in the world Melissa wanted to do was follow. Unfortunately, she knew it was the first thing Sean wanted.

"C'mon," he whispered.

(See what I mean?)

Melissa hesitated. She had lots of things planned for her life, and dying was not one of them.

"Will you c'mon!" Sean scowled and waved for her to follow.

Reluctantly, Melissa obeyed. But not before uttering the words that had become her trademark on nearly every case: "All right, but if we die, you're going to live to regret it."

They followed the old man down the hall and into the deserted sanctuary. It was pretty dark and spooky, with more than the usual amount of creaky boards, sticky cobwebs, and scurrying critter feet.

They continued through the sanctuary until they arrived at the front of the building. Then the old man turned and started to climb up the steep steps to the belfry.

Sean swallowed hard. He took a deep breath, and

with a heavy sigh began to climb. Melissa did the same, but with a much heavier sigh.

They had nearly reached the top when Sean figured it might be a good idea to ask a question or two. "Where exactly are you taking us?" he asked. "Is this where you live . . . up here in the belfry? Are you the one responsible for all those flickering lights that people—"

Suddenly he came to stop. For as he stepped into the small room at the top of the stairs, he saw their old buddy Spalding.

"Oh no," Spalding groaned. "It's the Hunter brats."

But Spalding wasn't Sean's only surprise. For sitting beside Spalding on a broken-down sofa were his two sidekicks—KC, a rough-and-tumble tomboy (despite her tiny 4'6" height), and Bear, who was as big as KC was small, and as dumb as . . . well, let's just say he wouldn't be winning any scholarships to Harvard . . . or to Sesame Street, for that matter.

"What are you guys doing here?" Sean asked.

Spalding scorned, "I assume our purposes are identical. We are here to retrieve the pirate's treasure before Father destroys the premises."

Melissa cleared her throat, but before she could say anything, the old man broke into another cackling laugh.

"Ah, zee treazure, zee treazure. Zer iz treazure here, all right. Yez, zer iz."

Everyone grew silent, waiting for more. They weren't disappointed.

"But you muzt be very carevul. You muzt bevare ov . . ." He threw a nervous glance in both directions and then continued. "You muzt bevare ov . . . ZEEG REEED."

"Who?" Spalding asked.

"He iz not a who . . . he iz an it." The old man lowered his voice. "ZEEG REEED. He iz a ferociouz beazt whoz appetite iz never quenched. He vaits in zee shadows, zearching for hiz next victim to devour."

Suddenly the room grew very cold. No one said a word. Finally Melissa found her voice. "Who . . . who are you?" she ventured. "Are you a friend of this ZEEG REEED?"

The old-timer let out another cackling laugh. "ZEEG REEED iz nobody'z vriend." With that, he turned to a beat-up suitcase on the floor, one that he'd been packing.

"But . . . who are you?" Melissa repeated.

He gave no answer as he resumed stuffing ragged clothes and odds and ends into the suitcase.

"He's just some homeless bum," KC sneered. Her

voice had the delicate sound of sandpaper rubbing over broken glass.

Spalding nodded in agreement. "I advised him to vacate the premises before Father's purchase of the church tomorrow and its subsequent demolition."

"Zat's right," the old man cackled. "I am geetting out vhile zee getting iz good. And I vould advize you to do zee zame. Geet out vile you ztill can." He slammed the suitcase shut and clutched it to his chest.

His eyes wildly scanned the belfry one last time until he suddenly broke out laughing. "But you von't. You vill ztay and zeek zee treasure . . . until you—" he pointed a crooked finger at each of them—"until you are all deztroyed, until each and every one of you is devoured by ZEEG REEED." After another cackling laugh, he turned and headed for the steps. "ZEEG REEED, ZEEG REEED . . ." he called as he moved down the stairs. "Bevare of ZEEG REEED!"

And then, just like that, he was gone.

FRIDAY, 08:00 PDST

The following morning it was Sean's turn to fix breakfast, which meant charcoal-burnt toast topped with chunks of frozen butter, along with cold cereal in dirty bowls. His speciality.

"So," Dad said, staring at a mound of Fruity Flakes piled before him. "At least you know the light in the belfry was from a homeless person living there."

Melissa nodded. "But we're still not sure where all that wailing and moaning comes from." She tried to slip Slobs her burnt toast under the table, but the dog was too smart to fall for it.

"And there's still that treasure," Sean added as he sat down to join them. "I mean, that's the main reason we're going back today, because of the treasure."

"I don't know if that's such a good idea," Dad said skeptically.

"Think of all that money we could be getting," Sean insisted.

"That's exactly what I am think—"

"We could become millionaires overnight. We could get Bloodhounds, Inc. all sorts of cool stuff. Buy whatever we want for the house, a couple big screen TVs for my room. Shoot, we might even take *you* out for dinner sometime."

"As long as it's Senior Discount Night," Melissa teased.

Dad gave her a look, then grinned.

"But we can't do any of that stuff if you won't let us find the treasure," Sean said.

Dad took a deep breath and looked out the window. Melissa knew these types of decisions were hard for him to make. Ever since they'd lost their mother to cancer a few months ago, he didn't like for any of them to take chances.

But Sean, in his usual insensitivity, didn't notice. Instead, he'd begun his world famous begging routine. "Please," he whined. "Just think what we could do with all that money, with all that wonderful, cold, hard cash."

"Easy, Sean," Melissa said, "you're drooling worse than Slobs."

"Hey, it doesn't hurt to want stuff."

"Maybe it does," Dad said as he finally looked back to him.

"What do you mean?"

Dad shrugged. "The love of riches can be a pretty dangerous thing."

"There's nothing wrong with being rich, is there?" Melissa asked.

"I didn't say being rich was wrong," Dad answered. "But the love *for* riches, that's what can be dangerous. In fact, it was Jesus himself who said, 'Be on your guard against all kinds of greed.' "

"Jesus said that?" Melissa asked.

"That doesn't make sense," Sean said.

"It does if you realize that greed can do weird things to you."

"How so?" Melissa questioned.

"I've seen it make good folks bad and loving people hateful. I've actually seen it ruin lives."

"Really?" Melissa asked.

Dad nodded. "The Bible says that real riches, life's real treasures, lie in being friends with God. But I've seen the love for money take people's eyes off God until getting rich became the only thing that was important to them."

"You don't have to worry about that happening to us," Sean said.

Melissa turned to him with a smirk. "Is that why you practically got us killed last night?"

"What?"

"You said yourself that the treasure was the only reason we went to the church last night."

"That was only part of it," Sean argued.

Melissa gave him a look.

"What about all those weird sounds?" he asked. "Shouldn't we be investigating those, too? Hmm? And what about this ZEEG REEED guy? He sounds pretty mysterious."

"And deadly."

"We're a detective agency, Misty. These are exactly the type of mysteries we're supposed to be solving."

Melissa shook her head. "The only mystery is how you and I could possibly be related."

"All right," Dad said, holding up a hand. "That's enough, now."

"So can we go back and investigate?" Sean asked.

Dad hesitated, then answered. "I'm not saying you can't . . ."

"All right!" Sean cried.

"But I *am* saying you have to be careful. Be very careful on this one, guys."

"Of course!" Sean exclaimed. "You know us." Then before Dad could say that's what he was worried about, Sean turned to Melissa

"You hear that?" he asked. "We can go ahead with the investigation."

Melissa cranked up a pathetic excuse for a smile. "Oh boy," she sighed, "I can hardly wait. . . ."

43

4

Dropping In for a Look

"Thanks for letting us borrow these X-ray goggles," Sean said as he, Melissa, and Slobs entered through the back door of the church. "They'll come in handy if that treasure really is hidden inside one of the walls."

"No problem-o," little Jeremiah squeaked from inside Melissa's digital watch. " 'Do unto others before the early bird gets the worm,' that's what I always say."

Despite her fear, Melissa couldn't help giggling. "Actually, the saying goes—"

WOOOooooooo . . .

Suddenly there was no need to correct him. Come to think of it, there was no need to do anything but shiver.

45

"Wh-h-hat was that?" Jeremiah stuttered.

"We're not sure," Sean whispered as they moved through the hall and cautiously entered the sanctuary. "Could be that ZEEG REEED character."

"That what?" Jeremiah squeaked.

WOOO*oooooo* . . .

Sean waited until the sound died down. "The best we figure, it's some sort of monster or something." He tried to sound bored, but Melissa could tell her brother was as nervous as she was. "It probably guards the treasure and attacks those who are looking for it."

"It does what?" Jeremiah cried.

But before Sean could answer, Slobs began to growl.

"What's wrong, girl?" Melissa whispered. "Are you okay?"

The growl grew louder as Slobs looked toward the front of the sanctuary.

"Sean . . ." Melissa whispered, "take a look at Slobs."

"I see."

So did Jeremiah. His little voice crackled nervously from the watch. "Well, would you look at the time. I need to be getting a-short."

"You mean 'along,' " Melissa said. "But you just got here. What's the rush?"

WOOOoooooo . . .

"I, uh, that is to say, er, my socks! Yeah, that's it! I've got to wash my socks!"

"Jeremiah," she chided. "You're a computer-generated character. Computer characters don't wash socks—or even wear them, for that matter."

WOOOoooooo . . .

"So you're going to let a little thing like that stop me from running for my life?"

Melissa could only shake her head. Jeremiah was cute and funny. But the word "brave" had never been programmed into his data base. "Okay," she sighed, "if you gotta go, you gotta go."

Jeremiah gave her a thumbs-up. "You've got that left," he said as he faded from her watch. "Catch you ladder, dud."

Of course he meant, "Catch you later, dude," but he was gone before she could correct him. Which was okay because at the moment, Melissa had a few other things on her mind.

Like the constant wailing, Slobs' continual growling, and watching Sean nervously slip on the X-ray goggles to take a better look. Everything was fine until Sean suddenly yelled in surprise . . . which caused Slobs to suddenly bark in surprise . . . which caused Melissa to suddenly scream in surprise . . . which was more than enough surprises to go around.

"What is it?" Melissa cried. "What do you see? What do you see?"

Sean could only point to the front wall behind the altar.

Melissa directed her flashlight to it. There was nothing but the usual dust and cobwebs. "What?" she asked.

"It's . . . it's hollow," he stuttered. "The wall . . . it's hollow."

"Are you sure?"

He nodded. "There's some sort of space behind it—a passageway." He tilted his head down. "It runs under the floor right behind the altar there."

Without hesitating, he started toward it. The wood creaked and groaned under his weight.

"Sean, be careful," Melissa whispered. "That floor looks pretty rotten."

WOOOOOoooooooooooo . . .

The wailing grew louder.

"Sean . . ."

She knew he heard her, but she also knew that he was too curious to listen. She stayed glued to his side, keeping her light just a few feet ahead of them as they arrived at the altar and moved around it.

That's when she saw the spongy section of flooring. It was right between the altar and the front wall.

"Sean," she warned.

"I've never seen anything like it," he whispered as he continued forward. "It looks like a tunnel or—"

"Sean, the floor!"

WOOOOOOOOOOOooooooooooo . . .

"*Sean!*" She reached out to grab his arm. "*Sean, don't step*—"

But she was too late. His foot hit the dark, soggy wood, and a moment later he was falling through it.

"AUGHhhhh . . ."

"Sean!" she screamed.

But he did not answer.

"Sean, can you hear me? Sean! Sean, answer me!"

49

If he answered, she could not hear. The wailing had suddenly grown deafening.

WOOOOOOOOOOOOOOOOOoooooooooooooooooo . . .

And with the deafening roar came the wind. A ferocious wind that flew up out of the hole and into her face, blowing her hair in all directions, screaming into her ears.

"*Sean!*" she shouted. "*Sean!*"

And then she saw the briefest movement of shadow. "*Sean?!*"

She dropped to her hands and knees. Cautiously, she approached the gaping hole, careful not to fall through it herself. She shined the flashlight down into the darkness.

"*SEAN?*"

Nothing but the wind and the wailing.

"*SEAN, ARE YOU ALL RIGHT? SEAN?*"

And then, ever so slowly, the howling began to die down.

"Sean . . ."

Eventually her light caught a glimpse of him. He was a good eight to ten feet away, under the floorboards, directly beneath the front wall.

"Sean?"

"I'm all right," he answered. He started to rise. "It's a tunnel. Some sort of passageway."

Melissa craned her neck for a better look.

"That's where the sound is coming from," he said. "The howling—it's the wind whipping through this tunnel."

"A tunnel?" Melissa repeated. "But where does it go to? If there's wind, it must be coming from some—" Suddenly an icy dampness touched her arm. She screamed and spun the flashlight around to see . . .

. . . Slobs, giving her arm a sniff. The poor animal yelped and leaped back in terror.

"Oh, sorry, girl," Melissa said as she reached out to pet the dog. "I'm sorry."

Slobs gave a pathetic whine and drew closer, obviously milking the sympathy for all she could.

"Shine your light back down here," Sean called. "Misty?"

Melissa turned back to the hole and shone the flashlight inside.

"More," he ordered. "I need more light."

She obeyed. The floor groaned slightly as she inched a little closer to the opening.

"More."

She stretched another inch, maybe two . . . which was about two inches farther than she should have. Suddenly the floor gave way, and she tumbled through the opening after her brother.

"AUGHHhhh . . ."

But unlike Sean's fall, this one seemed to last forever. And when she finally did hit—"OAFF!"—it wasn't just once, but again, "OAFF! OAFF!" and again, "OAFF! OAFF! OAFF!" It was as if she was bouncing down stairs. When she finally stopped (which was a good thing because she'd just about run out of "OAFFs"), she was pretty bruised and shaken. But as far as she could tell, nothing was broken.

The ground felt damp and cold. Not at all like the floorboards of the church.

"Misty?" Sean's voice came from somewhere up above. "Misty, are you all right? Misty, are you down there?"

She took a ragged breath. "Yeah . . . I'm okay," she called.

She heard Sean scrambling down after her. With him came a few hundred pounds of lose dirt and rock.

"Are you sure?" he asked as he reached her side.

"Yeah," she said, coughing. "Where . . . are we?"

"I figure we're 'bout fifteen feet under the church."

"Fifteen feet!"

"Yeah, you found a bunch of steps cut out in the dirt. Looks like they lead under the church and out toward a tunnel."

"Wonderful," she groaned.

"Shh . . ." He motioned for her to be quiet. "Listen . . ."

Melissa strained to hear. Directly above them was some sort of noise. Like someone pacing the floor.

"What's that?" Melissa whispered.

Sean gave no answer.

Suddenly more dirt and rock began showering down on them.

"Something's coming after us," Sean cried.

The noise increased. The mini-avalanche continued. Whatever it was, it was heading down the steps, and it was big. Real big.

Melissa braced herself. Her mind filled with a thousand thoughts, each and every one involving the ZEEG REEED coming to devour them. She wanted to run, to get away, but she was torn between scrambling to her feet and running down an unknown tunnel or turning to face an unknown monster.

(Decisions, decisions. Sometimes it's hard deciding which way to die.)

The creature was practically on top of them now.

"Who are you?!" Sean shouted into the darkness. "What do you want?! Who are—"

And then the thing hit. Hard.

It knocked them both to the ground. Sean yelled and Melissa screamed.

But only for a second. That was all it took before the wet, slobbery tongue started covering Melissa's face with drooling licks.

"Slobs," she coughed, trying to push the dog away as she caught her breath. "Slobs get off, girl. Get off. Slobs, get off *now*!"

After a little more coaxing, the big dog finally clambered off her—all 102 pounds' worth.

"Well, that was exciting," Melissa said as she wiped the slick drool from her face. "What's next? An earthquake? An attack by Martians? How about—"

"A hundred red eyes staring at us?" Sean offered.

"What?" She glanced at her brother. Like her, he was still on his hands and knees. Only now he was staring straight ahead. She followed his gaze. At first she saw nothing. But as she squinted, the things came into focus.

Faint at first. Very faint. Still, there was just enough light spilling down through the hole to illuminate them.

Or at least their eyes. . . .

Hundreds of them, maybe more. All beady, all red, and all less than three feet from her own face.

Melissa gasped and scampered back in terror. She fumbled to turn on her flashlight. It was blinding, stabbing her eyes.

It didn't do much for the hundred beady little ones, either. The hundred beady little eyes that were suddenly filled with panic as their little feet and little claws began scampering this way and that.

At last Melissa's own eyes adjusted to the light. She wished they hadn't.

"RATS!" she screamed. "We're in a nest of rats!"

5

ZEEG REEED Closes In . . .

FRIDAY 09:00 PDST

Normally, Sean liked being a guy. Yes sir, nothing beats messy rooms, giving wedgies, belching in public, and all the other hundred and one things guys can get away with that girls can't. But right now he would have given anything to join Melissa in her screaming-girl routine. Something about a bazillion rodents scurrying all over you can make screaming your lungs out kinda popular. But since screaming is not in the *Official Guys' Handbook* (probably written by the same person who wrote the *Big Brother's Handbook* back in chapter two), Sean had to settle for the next best thing. . . .

Shaking in his boots, trying to catch his breath. And of course the ever popular

"AGHHHHHHHHHHHHHHHHHHHHHHHHHHHH!!!!"
(Please note, this is not screaming.
Yelling, perhaps. Shouting, sure.
But it is definitely not girl-type screaming.)
Good. Now that we've got *that* straightened out . . .

It was hard to imagine who was more frightened:
Sean, Melissa, Slobs . . . or the rats. But when the yelling,
barking, squeaking, and yes, screaming were all over, the
brother and sister had dashed fifty yards farther down
the tunnel.

When Sean finally came to a stop, he leaned against
the tunnel wall trying to catch his breath. "Boy, was that
fun," he gasped in obvious sarcasm. "We'll have to do
that again real soon."

"Yeah," Melissa agreed, also gulping in air, "like the
year 2099."

Sean nodded, then glanced around. "Where's Slobs?"

"I don't know." Melissa snapped the flashlight back
on. "Slobs . . . where are you, girl? Slobs?" She scanned
the tunnel with the beam. The dirt and clay sides
glistened with moisture. She threw a look over her
shoulder. The entrance, with its steep dirt steps, was no
longer visible.

Now there was only darkness. She turned and shined the light in front of them.

More tunnel and more darkness.

"Slobs?" Sean called. "Slobs, where are you, girl? Slobs?"

But there was no answer. Only the wind as it whistled through the tunnel.

"You think she ran back?" Melissa asked.

Sean shrugged. "Could've. I tell you, sometimes I think that dog is more chicken than hound."

"Maybe," Melissa answered, "but she can also sense stuff we can't." With that, she turned and started back toward the church.

Sean grabbed her arm. "You're not going back?"

"Of course I am."

"Why would you want to do something like that?"

"Oh, I don't know . . ." Melissa pretended to think. "Maybe it has something to do with living."

"But we've gone this far. What about the treasure?"

"Sean . . ."

"Don't you get it?" he said. "The rumors *were* true. There *was* something behind the church walls. *This tunnel.*"

Melissa started to pull away, but he tightened his

grip. "And if the rumors were true about this tunnel, then they'll be true about the treasure. It's all connected. This tunnel will lead us to the treasure. I'm sure of it."

"Sean . . ."

"C'mon, Misty, think of what we can do with all that money. Think of all the stuff we can buy. We could redecorate your room. Shoot, we could buy you a whole new room. We could buy a whole new house . . . for each of us."

But even as he spoke Sean felt a little uneasy. Something about Dad's lecture on greed kept rattling around inside his head. Still, he could see Melissa starting to weaken, so he pressed on. "Dad wouldn't have to work day and night to keep the radio station going. We could buy it flat out. We could buy lots of radio stations. In fact, we could buy just about anything we wanted."

He could see her hesitate. She looked back down the tunnel. He had her. He knew it.

"How much farther do you think this goes?" she asked.

"I don't know. The best I figure, we're under the cemetery now, so—"

"*UNDER the cemetery?*" Melissa cried as she looked up to the ceiling.

"Yeah, from what I figure."

"You mean, the caskets and dead people and all that stuff . . . they're above us?"

"Well, uh—" Sean cleared his throat—"yeah, I guess." Now it was his turn to look nervously up at the ceiling.

Melissa slowly turned to Sean.

Sean slowly turned to Melissa.

Maybe Slobs was right after all.

YEEEEOOOOOOOWWWWWWWwwwww . . .

Suddenly an unearthly scream roared behind them. Part human, part they-didn't-know-what. It came from the church entrance and reverberated along the walls of the tunnel. Then came another

AAAOOOOOOOWWWWWWWlllllll . . .

"It's ZEEG REEED!" Melissa gasped.

Sean squinted back into the darkness. "Maybe . . . then again, maybe—"

But there was no time for maybes. Suddenly Slobs emerged from the darkness, heading directly toward them. If she had wanted to go back to the church, she had definitely changed her mind. Now she was baying and running for all she was worth.

"It's ZEEG REEED!" Melissa cried. "Run, Sean! Run!"

They took off as Slobs zoomed past them. Another anguished cry echoed through the tunnel. Cemetery or no cemetery, Sean and Melissa ran underneath it as fast as their terrified tootsies could take them.

Melissa tried to keep the flashlight beam ahead of them so they wouldn't trip over any stray rocks or boulders.

"OUCH, OW, OO, OUCH!"

But she didn't always succeed. Even though the light pointed at the floor, she couldn't help noticing the reflection of white roots now jutting out from the roof and sides of the tunnel. At least she hoped they were white roots. After what Sean had said about the cemetery above them, she wasn't so sure.

It's not that Melissa was afraid of dead people. Dad had cleared that up long ago. During their first couple of cases, he'd quoted the Bible more than once: *"Absent from the body, present with the Lord."*

The meaning was simple: Dead souls do not hang around graveyards. When people die, they go to face God. No stopping by seances for special guest appearances, no dropping by haunted houses to give folks a little scare.

And Melissa believed this . . . for the most part. It's just that, well, at least at this particular moment, she didn't feel a strong desire to stop and check to see if those white tree roots really were white tree roots.

Besides, there was the other problem. The one that started with the word ZEEG and ended with the word REEED. As they ran, they could no longer hear the creature behind them, but they knew it was still there. It was still pursuing them. Something like that doesn't just scream in darkened tunnels and scare children and bloodhounds senseless for the fun of it. It had a reason. And the reason the old homeless fellow had given them made perfect sense:

"He vaits in zee shadows, searching vor hiz next victim. . . ."

Then, of course, there was the added little treat:

"You vill be deztroyed . . . you vill all be devoured by ZEEG REEED."

Other than that, there was really no reason to be

running for their lives down a pitch-black tunnel under a graveyard. No reason at all.

Suddenly that pitch-black tunnel took a hard left.

Well, the tunnel did. Unfortunately, Melissa and Sean didn't.

The turn was too sharp, and the floor was too slick. They both slid out of control. But only for a second.

K-Splat, K-Splat.

That was the sound of two soft bodies hitting the wall of a very wet and not-so-soft tunnel.

K-Thud, K-Thud.

Same bodies, only now they'd fallen to the floor.

Melissa was the first to speak. "Sean . . ." she groaned. "Sean, will you get off of me!"

"I'm trying," he said as he struggled to stand. "But my shirt, it's all tangled up. It's caught in this, in this . . ."

"In what?" she asked.

"I don't know. Some sort of white tree root or something."

Melissa gave a swallow. She could have gone a whole day without hearing that. "Are you sure it's a tree root?" she asked.

"What else could it be?" he asked as he kept trying to untangle himself. "It's white and long and—hey, that's weird."

"What's weird?" Melissa asked, not really wanting to know.

"This root."

"What about it?"

"What's a white tree root doing with a ring on one of its . . . hey, Misty?"

"Yes, Sean."

"Tree roots don't have fingers, do they?"

"I don't think so, Sean."

"So if this has fingers, then it isn't a tree root."

"Probably not, Sean."

"And if it's not a tree root, then it's . . ."

They both had the answer at the same time.

"A SKELETON!"

Melissa leaped to her feet. Now she did what she was becoming a pro at. She ran. Like the wind. A moment later, Sean had joined her side. Together, the two ran as fast as they could. Maybe even a little faster. Which wasn't too bad of an idea.

Well, except for the cavern.

Before they knew it, the tunnel opened up onto a

magnificent cavern. It was at least forty feet high and probably that deep. Multicolored stalactites glistened from the ceiling. It was breathtaking. The type of place Sean and Melissa could have really enjoyed

—if they hadn't suddenly run out of path.

—if that path hadn't ended on top of a thirty-foot cliff overlooking a raging river.

—if they hadn't suddenly shot off that path, over that cliff, and tumbled head over heels through the air toward that river.

"AUGHHHHHHHhhhhh . . ."

Other than that, they would have absolutely loved the place.

6

GLUG ... Glug ... glug

FRIDAY, 09:08 PDST

When we last left our herocs, they were once again doing what they did best.

"AUGHHHHHHhhhhhh ..."

The good news was that their screaming didn't last forever. They eventually splashed into the river. The bad news was it's hard to scream when you're busy drowning. Still, Melissa did manage to squeeze in a few cries.

"HELP..."
glug, glug, glug
"...I CAN'T..."

glug, glug, glug
" . . . SWIM!"

Sean would have joined her, but he was too busy spinning underneath the water. It seems he was caught in some type of current. The poor guy tumbled around so many times he didn't know which way was up. He knew there was a surface—he just didn't know where to find it. Not a big problem, except for the breathing part. It seems he hadn't done that in quite a while. And since breathing air is a lot more fun than breathing water, he took a wild guess where the surface might be and swam toward it.

Not a bad idea until

BONK!

He hit the bottom of the river. Now at least he knew where the surface was *not*. He tucked his legs under and pushed off. A moment later he shot to the surface, coughing and choking for air . . . until he heard

"Sean . . . help me . . . help . . ."

He spun around and spotted Melissa. She was downriver twenty yards, desperately clinging to a large boulder.

"Hang on!" he shouted. "I'm coming. Hang on!"

He swam toward her for all he was worth. It made no difference that Melissa's bedroom was twice as big as his and that if anything ever happened to her he'd probably get it. And it didn't matter that if she was gone he might actually get into the bathroom sometime before noon.

None of these things counted to Sean. After all, that was his sister there, and she needed his help (although it was a good thing he didn't remember the cool stereo of hers he would have also gotten).

Thanks to the swift current and his great swimming abilities, Sean quickly raced toward her. "Hang on," he shouted. "I'll save you! I'll save you!"

"Sean . . ."

"Hang on!"

"Sean!"

"Hang on."

"Sean, you're coming too fast! Sean!"

But Sean was too busy being a hero to pay any attention to details. "Hang on!"

"Slow down! Sean, you're going to—"

K-RASH . . .

The good news was Sean had gotten to his sister before she drowned.

The bad news was he smashed into her so hard that she lost her grip on the rock. Now they were both being swept away by the current.

Unfortunately, Sean wasn't done being a hero. Not yet.

"Grab hold of me!" he shouted.

"What?" Melissa cried, coughing, trying to keep her head above water.

"Grab hold of me! I'll save you."

She threw him a look. "Haven't we already tried that?"

"Just grab hold of me, will you!"

"Sean, I really don't think—"

Suddenly the current dragged her under. "Ah . . ."

"Misty!" he cried.

But she was nowhere to be seen.

"MISTY?"

A moment later she popped up behind him, gagging and coughing.

"Misty!"

"Present," she gasped.

"Will you stop being so stubborn and grab hold of me!"

Melissa had taken in too much water to argue. She reached out to her brother just as she started going under again. But instead of grabbing his arm or shoulder, she grabbed his neck.

"Mis—" he choked. "Misty, I can't breathe! Mis—"

But at the moment she was too busy drowning to listen.

"Mis—"

She squeezed his throat harder until she wound up dragging both of them under water. Wonderful—now Sean had to decide which was better, being choked to death or drowned to death. Decisions, decisions.

But there was one other choice he hadn't considered. . . .

Suddenly they were both out of the water. It was as if God himself had snatched them from the jaws of death. As if some supernatural force had dragged them out of the water and into the fresh, wonderful, breathable air.

Well, that was one explanation. Unfortunately, there was another. . . .

Sean hovered in the air, absolutely amazed . . . until he looked down. Now he understood. They hadn't left

71

the river. The river had left them. It had dropped off into a beautiful cascading waterfall. A waterfall that splashed into a lovely pool fifty feet below. A lovely pool that they were now plunging headfirst into.

Sean looked to Melissa and shrugged. "Here we go again!"

She nodded, then joined him in what they did best.

"AUGHHHHHHHHHHHhhhhhhhhh . . ."

Sean was the first to hit the water. He was also the first to be knocked unconscious. But never wanting to be left out, Melissa soon followed.

Neither was exactly dead, but neither would be doing any more shouting for a while.

FRIDAY, 09:36 PDST

The first thing Sean remembered was someone tenderly caressing his face with a soft, damp cloth. It was so gentle that it reminded him of when Mom used to dab his fevered forehead with a moist washcloth. Keeping his eyes closed, Sean turned his face toward the tender person and sighed in appreciation.

The tender person whimpered an answer.

It was an odd response, and for a moment Sean thought of opening his eyes. But the gentle stroking felt so good that he pushed the thought from his mind and let out another relaxing sigh.

This time the answer came back as a whine . . . followed by a sharp bark.

Sean's eyes exploded open.

There was Slobs, straddled over him. That was no washcloth. It was a tongue! One very long, wet tongue smothering his face with concerned licks . . . and, of course, slobbers.

"Slobs!" he cried.

Thrilled over Sean's sudden recovery, Slobs licked him even harder.

"Slobs—"

. . . and drooled on him even more.

Sean coughed, trying to come up for air. "Slobs, please . . ." At last he was able to push the animal aside.

"Welcome back," Melissa said.

Sean rose up on his elbow to look around. Pain stabbed through his temples. "Ow!"

"You bumped your head pretty good when we landed," she said.

He winced as he touched the sides of his head. "What

73

about you?" he asked. "Are you okay?"

"You mean besides falling through a church floor . . . and being chased by some monster who wants to eat us . . . and being attacked by a skeleton . . . and falling into a river . . . and nearly drowning . . . and shooting off a waterfall?" She shrugged. "Yeah, other than that, I'm doing just fine."

Sean nodded. He got the point.

But Melissa wasn't quite done. "So tell me again, why are we doing all of this?"

Sean looked at her, then shrugged sheepishly. Of course she was right. They had gone through a lot of trouble, and for what? For some treasure that they hadn't even seen, that they weren't even sure was there? Right now it seemed more than a little stupid. What had Dad said? *"Greed can take over people's lives."* Well, he got that one right. Not only had greed taken over their lives, but it had almost stopped their lives.

"Hey, guys, what's going off?"

Sean glanced over at Melissa's watch. There was Jeremiah, complete with his neon red hair and electronic suit with patterns that kept shorting out, from stripes to plaids to polka dots, then to all three at the same time.

"Nothing much is happening here," Melissa sighed.

"Just another one of Sean's guided tours through Absurd-ville."

"Oh," Jeremiah said, glancing around, "so that's where we are."

"Actually," Sean corrected, "we're somewhere underground. But I have no idea where. I think we're, you know, kinda . . . lost."

Melissa shot him a look. "*Kinda* lost?"

"Hey," he argued, "we wouldn't be in this mess if you hadn't tried to drown me."

"Me?" Melissa protested. "I'm not the one who wanted to go on this crazy—"

"Kids, kids, kids." Jeremiah held out his hands. "There's no use crying over spilled Pepsi. I'll just check the coordinates and give you your location as quick as a drink."

Before Melissa could correct him, Jeremiah began his calculations. There was a series of flickers and flashes on her digital watch, along with plenty of

Beeps, Bops, Blimps, and B-U-R-P-S.

"Excuse me," Sean asked. "Was that a burp?"

"Sorry," Jeremiah shrugged. "Too much Pepsi."

More seconds passed as more calculations were made

75

until finally Jeremiah cried out, "I've got it!"

"I hope it's not contagious," Melissa mumbled.

"No, I've got it," Jeremiah repeated. "And, Sean, you were absolutely right."

"I was?" Sean asked in astonishment.

"Yup," Jeremiah nodded. "It's just like you said . . . you're lost."

Sean, Melissa, and this time even Slobs let out a groan.

"But there's a bright side," Jeremiah continued. "According to the wind velocity, saline concentration in the atmosphere, and barometric pressure, my guess is that you're very close to the ocean. In fact, that cave behind you will most likely lead out to the beach."

Sean and Melissa turned to look into the darkened cave behind them.

"Are you sure?" Sean asked.

"You bet. That's one chicken you can count before it crosses the road."

Sean began to nod. "That would make sense. If there really were pirates and they really did use that church, then this tunnel could have connected them right to—"

YEEEOOOOOOWWWWWWwwww . . .

Everyone spun around. The sound came from the top of the waterfall. It was an old familiar cry. One Sean was growing less and less fond of.

"Wh-wh-who's that?" Jeremiah stuttered.

"I'm afraid it's not a who," Sean said, squinting, trying to see through the mist. "It's a what."

"You don't mean. . . ?" Jeremiah asked.

Melissa nodded. "I'm afraid so." Already her voice was starting to quiver. "It's ZEEG REEED . . . and he's still coming after us!"

As if proving her point, the air was suddenly filled with

AAAOOOOOOWWWWllllll . . .

Melissa stepped closer to Sean, who started digging into his pack. Quickly, he pulled out the X-ray goggles. They were pretty wet and beat up.

"What are you doing with those?" she demanded.

"They'll let me see through the mist and rocks up there. Maybe I can spot whatever it is coming after us." He began to slip them on.

"Sean . . ." Melissa looked back over her shoulder at the cave. "Sean, we *know* how to get out of here. Let's go."

77

But her brother remained unmoving as he adjusted the focus on the goggles. "Where's your sense of wonder?" he asked. "Of curiosity?"

"Where's your sense of survival?" she demanded. "Come on!"

But Sean continued adjusting the goggles until a form finally came into view. It was dark and menacing as it raced toward the edge of the falls. Any moment now it would shoot over the top and come swooping down at them.

"Got it," he announced. "Now if only . . . uh-oh."

"What do you see?" Melissa cried. "What does it look like?"

Sean continued to stare. "I can't tell for certain, but—" Suddenly he stopped.

"But what?" Melissa asked. "What do you see?"

"It's . . ." Sean swallowed hard. "It has . . . six legs."

"Six legs?!" Melissa shouted.

Sean nodded. "And at least that many arms and . . ."

"And what?" she cried.

"And three heads!"

7

The More the Merrier

FRIDAY, 10:04 PDST

The ZEEG REEED appeared over the edge of the waterfall and started its downward plunge. True to form, it let out one unearthly screech:

YEEEOOOOOWWWWWWwwwww . . .

Followed by the other:

AAAOOOOOOWWWWWWllllll . . .

But as Melissa watched the creature fall, its six arms, six legs, and three heads started to look familiar. And the closer it came, the more familiar they looked. One of the heads sort of resembled Spalding, the spoiled rich kid. Another could have passed for KC, the tomboy. And the third almost looked like their burly friend, Bear.

At least that's who they kind of looked like as they splashed into the water. But when they popped back up to the surface, that's *exactly* who they looked like. It wasn't the ZEEG REEED creature, but the kids. Unfortunately, there was little time to celebrate since, at the moment, they were busy drowning!

"*Help us,*" they shouted. "*Help . . .*"

Without stopping to think, Sean raced to the water's edge. He was about to dive in when Melissa grabbed his arm. "You can't go back in there!" she shouted. "The current is too swift."

"*Help . . . somebody, help . . .*"

Sean glanced at the water. She was right, of course. The current was far too strong. Suddenly he had another idea. "Grab my hand," he ordered.

"What?"

"Take my hand. I'll wade in to try to snag them when they pass."

"Sean—"

"If we don't help them, they'll drown!"

"*Help . . . please . . . somebody . . .*"

Melissa hesitated only a moment before nodding. She grabbed her brother's hand as he waded into the water.

The current was strong. She could see him fighting to keep his balance as she held on tightly.

He called out to them, "This way! The current's coming toward me. Swim into it and I'll catch you!"

KC was the first to obey. She swam until she entered the current. It grabbed her and quickly pulled her toward him until

"Oaff!"

He got her. (Or she got him.) Melissa reached out to KC with her free hand and pulled her to shore, where she stumbled to her knees and then collapsed onto the sand.

Next came Spalding. He also caught the current and was also slammed into Sean, but a lot harder.

"OAFF!"

And finally, Bear.

"AUGH!"
K-RUNCH.

The "AUGH!" was Sean screaming as he saw the mountain of a boy racing toward him. The *K-RUNCH* was Sean's body when the mountain of a boy smashed into him.

A few moments later everyone was lying on the beach. And after their daily minimum requirement of coughing and gasping, they were finally able to start figuring out what had happened.

"Was that you screaming on top of the waterfall?" Melissa asked.

"Naw," KC scorned. "I'm not the screaming type . . . that was Spalding and Bear."

Spalding and Bear nodded sheepishly.

"What about the tunnel?" Sean asked. "When we were under the cemetery, we heard the same yelling.

"That was us, too," Bear admitted.

"Back when we fell through the floor of the church," Spalding added.

"So all the screaming was coming from you guys and not the ZEEG REEED?" Melissa asked.

They nodded.

"However," Spalding said, "that does not imply that the ZEEG REEED is no longer in our vicinity. There is still a high probability that he is searching for us." Spalding lowered his voice and glanced around.

"Needless to say, you recall what that homeless wretch at the church said. The creature's sole purpose is to devour all those who seek the treasure."

A moment of silence crept over the group. Silence—and goose bumps.

"So what are we supposed to do?" KC complained. "Just hang around, waitin' to become some monster's after-school snack?"

Melissa shook her head. "Jeremiah says that cave behind us is a way out. He says it leads out to the beach."

"Who's Jeremiah?" KC demanded.

"Oh," Melissa smiled. "He's this little guy on my watch."

"You got a talking watch?"

"No, he's just this—well, here, see for yourself." Melissa held out her wrist. "His name is Jeremiah. Actually, it's J.E.R.E.M.I.A.H., which is short for the Johnson Electronic Reductive Entity Memory Inductive Assembly Housing, and as you can see he . . ." Melissa slowed to a stop.

All three faces stared at her skeptically.

"What's wrong?" she asked.

"There ain't nobody in there," KC said.

"Don't be silly," Melissa answered, glancing at her watch. "Of course he's—"

She came to another stop. They were right. Jeremiah was no longer there. "Well," she chuckled nervously, "he *was* here."

She glanced up. They continued staring. Melissa felt her face growing a little hot around the edges. "Sometimes, though," she nervously cleared her throat, "sometimes he's kinda shy. Fact, Sean and I are about the only ones he ever talks to. Isn't that right, Sean?"

They turned to her brother.

He stared at her, pretending to be clueless.

"Sean?" she said.

He looked at her blankly. Then he blinked. "Yes, dear sister?"

"Jeremiah," she insisted. Her words grew more pointed. "Tell them about Jeremiah."

Again he pretended ignorance. Then suddenly his face lit up. "Oh yes, right . . . Jeremiah. Jeremiah usually stays with us, but right now he's hanging out with the Easter Bunny and the Tooth Fairy."

"Sean!"

"Yeah," Sean nodded, continuing to make her look the fool (one of his favorite pastimes). "They're all up at the North Pole giving Santa Claus and his elves a hand for Christmas."

KC and Spalding exchanged scornful snickers.

Melissa's face grew hotter. "*SEAN!*"

"But she's right about one thing," he said. "This cave is our only way out."

"How can you be so certain?" Spalding asked.

Sean shrugged. "After calculating the wind velocity, saline concentration of the atmosphere, and the barometric pressure, the fact becomes quite obvious."

Spalding slowly nodded. "Of course."

KC and Bear nodded, pretending to look like they understood.

But not Melissa. She wore an entirely different expression. In fact, if looks could kill, Sean would be a dead man.

"Then what are we waitin' for?" KC demanded. "Let's get outta here." Without another word, she got to her feet and headed for the cave.

The others rose and followed.

The cave was long and dark. Unlike the tunnel or the

cavern, the floor was filled with water . . . and it was getting deeper. Soon it was up to their calves, then their knees.

"You are certain this is the correct direction?" Spalding asked.

Sean stuck his hand down into the water, tasted it, then spit it out. "We're heading toward the ocean; this is definitely salt water."

"Excellent," Spalding answered.

"But we better hurry," Melissa said as she watched the water swirling around her legs. "Looks like the tide is coming in." The group continued forward. Well, most of the group.

"Where's Bear?" KC asked. She turned around. "Bear?"

Melissa shined her flashlight around the cave until she spotted him. The boy was a dozen feet behind them. He stood on a slight ledge, shining his own flashlight toward the ceiling.

"C'mon, Bear," she shouted. "The tide's coming in. We don't want to get trapped in here."

But Bear didn't answer. Instead, he continued to stand and stare.

"He's spotted something," KC said. She turned and

started back toward him. "What is it, Bear? What do you see?"

Spalding and Sean also turned back to investigate.

"Guys?" Melissa warned. "The tide is rising fast." But no one paid attention. Not even Slobs. Reluctantly, Melissa turned and sloshed back through the water to join them.

KC was the first to arrive. She followed Bear's gaze up toward the ceiling. That's when her mouth dropped open in astonishment.

Spalding joined her and did the same openmouthed routine.

And finally, Sean. "Will you look at that," he said in wonder.

At last Melissa arrived. She followed everyone's gaze. There was a shaft above them that veered sharply to the right. Up at the top was a type of ledge. And directly in the center of that ledge set a chest—three feet long, about half that wide, and made of metal. But not just any metal. By the blinding yellow reflection from their flashlights, it was obvious that this metal was nothing but pure gold. And attached to the gold were dozens of rubies, sapphires, and diamonds . . . each jewel reflecting and refracting their lights, filling the shaft with dazzling rainbows.

For a moment everyone stood in silence. Until finally Bear said what everyone else already knew.

"We found it!"

8

Shake, Rattle, and Rolled . . .

Friday, 10:21 PDST

It was hard to know exactly who had started the stampede toward the treasure. It really didn't matter. Because within half a second, everyone was clambering up the side walls of the shaft toward it . . . even Slobs. And the more they clamored, the pushier they got.

"Ouch! That's my hand."

"Get outta my way!"

"You're stepping on my face!"

"If you can't move it, lose it!"

"Stop pushin'!"

"Woof, woof, woof!"

Yes sir, greed was in full gear. Who cared how rude

they were? After all, that was a treasure up there! What difference did a few flattened heads, crushed ribs, and broken body parts make when compared to unlimited wealth.

Unfortunately, the rudeness had barely begun. Once they arrived at the chest, they began arguing over who the rightful owner should be.

"I was here first!"
　　"I saw it first!"
　　　　"I touched it first!"
　　　　　　"I grabbed the handle!"
　　　　　　　　"I grabbed the other handle!"
　　　　　　　　"Howl, howl, howl!"

No doubt about it, maturity was at a new low. We'll skip all the bickering and threats on one another's lives and just say that the argument went on and on. And just when you thought it was over, it went on some more. In fact, the words (not to mention barks and howls) were so heated that everyone missed two rather important facts.

FACT 1: The chest was wedged so tightly against the shaft's ceiling that it was actually holding part of it up.

FACT 2: The water in the tunnel below them
continued to fill with sea water.

Other than that, everything was fine and dandy.
Eventually, Sean managed to glance down.
"Uh, guys?" he called. "Guys!" No one listened.
"*GUUUYYYYYSSSS!*"
That got their attention.
"Didn't there use to be a tunnel below us?"
Everyone looked down.

The tunnel below them was rapidly filling with water.
In fact, there was less than three feet of space between
the tunnel's roof and the surface of the water. Make that
two feet, eight inches . . . er, two feet, five inches . . . er,
two feet—well, you get the picture.

So did the kids.

"We're all gonna drown!" Bear screamed.
"Let's get out of here!" KC shouted.

Once again the group moved along the sides of the
shaft, only this time in reverse. And once again they did
their usual arguing, bickering, and howling. Because if
there was one thing everybody loved more than money, it
was living.

Well . . . almost everybody. It seems Spalding hadn't

quite figured out the difference.

Melissa was the first to look up and spot him. He was still at the top of the shaft beside the chest. "Spalding, what are you doing?"

"It's imperative we not lose this wealth."

Melissa glanced down to the tunnel and the rising water. "We've got to get out of here!"

Spalding nodded as he grabbed a handle on the side of the chest and pulled. "I am painfully aware of that fact; however, one must at least attempt to—"

Sean was the first to see the dirt falling. "No!" he shouted. "Spalding, don't pull."

"And why not?"

"It's holding up the roof!"

"Nonsense," Spalding scoffed as he gave the chest another tug. More rock and dirt fell.

"Stop!" KC saw it, too. "Spalding, he's right! Stop!"

"If you think I am going to allow a little falling dirt to prevent me from obtaining this wealth, then you are sadly mistaken." He gave the chest another tug.

"Look out!" Sean yelled. Everyone ducked as more dirt and larger rocks fell.

"Spalding!" Melissa shouted. "Spalding, don't—"

But that was all she managed to get out before

Spalding gave the chest one final pull.

It came loose. And with it about ten tons of dirt and rock.

"Look out!" Bear cried.

"Avalanche!" Sean shouted.

The dirt and rocks cascaded down on top of them—smashing them, bruising them, quickly covering them. Over the roar of falling debris, everyone shouted and screamed. But Melissa only heard them for a moment . . . until one particularly nasty rock scored a direct hit on her noggin.

After that she heard nothing at all.

When she awoke, Melissa was half floating, half standing in thick brown goop. Either she'd fallen into a giant vat of liquid chocolate or the tunnel's dirt and water had mixed together forming a giant pit of mud. Unfortunately, she knew it was the latter.

The first person she spotted was KC. At least she thought it was KC. It was so dark, and the girl was so small and covered in mud that she could have just as easily passed for a chocolate-covered peanut with eyes.

"Are you all right?" Melissa called. KC gave no answer as she paddled toward her in the murky darkness.

"Are you okay?" Melissa repeated.

Still no answer.

"I said, are you—"

SLURP!

Suddenly KC licked Melissa's face and started to bark. And suddenly Melissa realized it was harder to recognize her mud-covered companions than she'd thought. "Slobs!" she cried.

The dog barked again and threw in a few more licks for good measure.

"Oh, there you are," Sean's voice called. Melissa turned and spotted somebody swimming toward her.

"Sean?" she asked.

"Who else?"

"I don't know," she said, wiping the dog drool from her mouth. "I just didn't want to take any more chances. Where are the others?"

"We're all here," the real KC answered from behind.

Melissa turned around in the gunk and saw another pair of eyes staring at her through the darkness.

"Where exactly is here?" she asked.

"We're still in the shaft," Bear's voice answered from the left.

Melissa glanced at him and then up to the roof. The ceiling was so close she could practically touch it. "That's impossible," she argued. "We've got less than two feet of head room, and the shaft was at least fifteen feet high."

Sean nodded. "That was before our friend Spalding here decided to fill it up with his little avalanche."

"I heard that," Spalding called from nearby. "I am only responsible for the dirt, not the mud. It is not my fault that this sea water keeps coming in from the, from the . . ."

Suddenly Melissa remembered. "From the rising tide!" She glanced at the side walls. It was true—even as she spoke, the water continued to rise and the breathing space above their heads continued to shrink. "There has to be some way out of here," she said nervously.

Sean shook his head. "I've looked. Our only escape was the tunnel below us, and now it's completely filled with mud and water."

"We're doomed," KC moaned.

"Not only that," Bear added, "but we ain't going to live too long, either."

Melissa glanced up at the ceiling. "How much time do you think we have?"

Sean watched the mud and water creep up the sides of the shaft. By now there was a little over a foot of air above their heads. "A minute," he said. "Maybe two."

Melissa let out a long sigh. "This was all my fault."

"What do you mean?"

"I should have never let you talk us into this."

Sean looked at her. Even in the darkness, he could see her sincerity. And it was then he knew that despite all the handbooks on big brotherhood, it was time to admit that he was actually wrong. "Nah," he said, shaking his head. "It was me."

Melissa looked at him. She was more than a little surprised. Come to think of it, so was Sean. But the honesty hadn't hurt too much, so he figured he'd keep going. . . .

"I'm the one who got us all caught up in looking for that treasure." He sighed heavily. "Dad was right . . . greed can really make you stupid."

Now it was Melissa's turn for honesty. "When you're right, you're right."

Sean gave her a look.

She smiled and shrugged. "Actually, I didn't have to

come with you. But I wanted to be rich as much as you. And now look where it got us. Dad said something else, too. Remember? Real riches can't be found in stuff—"

Sean finished the phrase, ". . . but in friendship with God." He gave another sigh. "And by taking our eyes off God, by looking for the wrong treasure . . . here we are."

Melissa nodded and sadly repeated. "Here we are."

"Shh . . ." Spalding suddenly whispered.

They turned to him.

He motioned toward the roof. "Up there. Listen."

Everyone strained to hear.

CLINK . . . SCRAPE.
CLINK . . . SCRAPE.

It was directly above their heads—the sound of metal against dirt. The sound of digging.

"Someone's up there!" KC shouted. "Someone's digging us out. Hey!" she cried. She began banging her little fists on the rocky ceiling. "Hey, we're down here!"

The others joined in. "WE'RE DOWN HERE! HELP US! WE'RE DOWN HERE!"

The digging grew louder. . . .

CLINK . . . SCRAPE.
CLINK . . . CLINK . . . SCRAPE.

97

. . . as the water surrounding them grew higher. Now there was less than a foot of air space. They were having to tilt their heads back just to keep the mud and water out of their mouths.

Sean had no idea how close the person rescuing them was or if he would even dig through to them in time. But remembering the X-ray goggles, he reached into his mud-drenched pack, found them, and slipped them on. They were cracked, full of gunk, and impossible to focus, but he adjusted them as best he could to try to see through the dirt and rock above.

What he saw made his blood run cold. There was some sort of form less than a foot above them. That was the good news. But there was some bad. . . .

It was hard to tell with the cracked and out-of-focus goggles, but the form had a strange outline. As if it were part human, part . . .

CLINK . . . CLINK . . . SCRAPE.
CLINK . . . SCRAPE.

Suddenly Sean understood. It was the creature. The one that had been chasing them. The one and only ZEEG REEED. It had finally sniffed them out. It had finally found them. And now that it had them trapped, it was closing in for the kill. . . .

q

ZEEG REEED

CLINK ... SCRAPE ... SCRAPE.
CLINK ... CLINK ... SCRAPE.

The shovel continued its digging until a blinding ray of light stabbed Melissa's eyes. There was more digging and more light. In a matter of seconds, a foot-wide hole of blazing daylight appeared above her.

It was a welcome sight. Particularly since the water was now up to her mouth. "Help me!" she coughed. "Help!" She reached her hand out of the hole. ZEEG REEED or no ZEEG REEED, she had to get out of there. They all had to get out of there.

More dirt was shoveled away. Clods and globs

splashed about her face. She looked up and could see him now, silhouetted against the sun. It was impossible to make out a face, but she was grateful to recognize a rough outline of something that could pass for human.

There were other clues that it might be a real person, like the old, weathered hand that suddenly thrust itself down to her.

And the voice.

"Jez take me hand, matey. Jez take old ov me hand."

Melissa recognized the accent instantly. She thought it odd that ZEEG REEED and the old man spoke with the same accent. Not only with the same accent, but in the exact same voice.

"Come on, ve haven't got all day."

Then it dawned on her. Maybe it wasn't ZEEG REEED after all. Maybe it was the old man instead. Marveling at her incredible intelligence, she took hold of the wrinkled hand and pulled with all of her might.

"My, iv you ain't zee heavy one," he groaned.

She hung on as he pulled until she finally came up out of the water and collapsed on the rocky shore. She could hear the surf pounding the jagged rocks less than a hundred feet away.

Still gasping for breath, she turned over to face him.

"You came back!" she cried. "You came back for us!"

"Iz a long ztory. I'll be happy to tell you, but giff me a hand vit your friendz virzt."

Melissa scampered to her knees just in time to see Sean's head appear out of the hole. He was squinting cautiously.

"It's okay," she shouted. "It's the old man from the church. Here, take our hands and we'll pull you out."

Sean didn't have to be asked twice. Melissa took one hand, and the old man took the other. With more than the usual amount of gruntings and groanings, they finally drug him out.

After a couple breaths, Sean rose to his feet. KC was the next to swim over to the hole. All three reached down and easily pulled her out.

After KC came Slobs, who was also easy (except for the thank-you licks she insisted on passing around to everybody).

Next came Bear.

Fortunately, with all four pulling (and Slobs barking in support), dragging him out wasn't as hard as they'd feared. It wasn't as easy, either. But what are a few broken backs and dislocated shoulders among friends?

"Zat iz all?" the old man asked, panting for breath.

"No," Melissa said. "Spalding is still down there."

The old man dropped to his knees. "I zee no Zpalding."

"He's down there," Melissa insisted. She joined his side, then lowered her head into the hole. "He has to be. He—" And then she spotted him—way off to the side. "There he is! Spalding!" she shouted. "Hurry. Come on out!"

"I have located the treasure chest," he called, barely able to keep his mouth above the water. "It was floating over by—"

"I don't care," Melissa interrupted. "Swim over to this opening and grab our hands so we can pull you out."

"But the chest, it is stuck under—"

"Will you swim over here!" she demanded.

Spalding tried to swim, stretching one way, then the other, but he would not let go of the chest, and the chest would not move.

Sean dropped his head down beside Melissa's. "What's the problem?"

"The chest," Spalding coughed. By now there were only a couple of inches of air and he was doing as much coughing and choking as he was breathing. "It is stuck.

"Let it go!" Sean shouted.

"Are you insane?" Spalding yelled. He coughed again, taking in more water.

"Spalding!" Melissa cried. "Let go of the chest!"

"Absolutely . . ." he coughed again, "not." Now even his face was disappearing under the water.

"Spalding!" Sean shouted. "You're going to drown. *Let go of the chest!*"

More coughing

"Spalding!"

"He won't let go!" Melissa cried. "He's drowning."

Sean dropped to his stomach and scooted farther into the hole. "Grab my feet," he ordered.

"What?"

"Take hold of my feet—I'm going in after him."

"Sean, don't be—"

"Just take hold of my feet!"

Melissa threw a glance to the old man.

"Grab my feet!" Sean demanded. "He's drowning!"

The old man nodded, and they both moved into action. They each took hold of one of Sean's legs. After a deep breath of air and a warning—"Whatever you do, don't let go"—Sean stuck his head into the water. It was followed by his shoulders, then his chest.

There was plenty of wiggling and squirming as he

stretched for the boy, and it was all Melissa could do to hang on. "Please, God," she whispered, "help me . . ."

It seemed Sean was down there forever until suddenly he started pulling back.

"He'z got 'im!" the old man shouted. "Pull, matey. Pull like you've never pulled bevore!"

Melissa nodded and tugged hard at Sean's legs. He seemed a lot heavier than before. She hoped it was because he had Spalding. At last Sean's shoulders appeared, then his neck, and finally his head. He came out gagging and choking, but at least he was breathing.

"I've got him," he coughed. "Keep pulling, I've got him." They nodded and kept tugging until, at last, Spalding's face came from the water. But unlike Sean, he wasn't breathing. And he was blue.

They quickly drug him out and onto the rocky shore.

"Spalding, can you hear me?" KC shouted. "Spalding, can you hear me?"

There was no answer.

"Is he. . . ?" Bear swallowed. "Is he croaked?"

"Not yet," the old man said. In one swift movement, he tilted back Spalding's head and pinched his nose. Then he placed his mouth over the boy's mouth and began forcing air into his lungs.

It only took two or three breaths before Spalding began coughing. The old man pulled away just as the kid coughed out a lungful of water. At last Spalding's eyes fluttered open. He tried to speak, but no words would come.

"It's okay," Melissa said. "You're okay."

He kept trying to talk until Melissa finally leaned toward him. She expected to hear some words of thanks, some deep, gut-wrenching emotion. Instead, she heard the gasped question: "Did we . . . get the . . . treasure?"

"Misty, look out!"

Melissa turned to Sean. He was pointing to the newly dug hole. It was starting to crumble around the edges. First a little, then a lot.

"It iz caving in!" the old man shouted.

Melissa didn't understand. "What?"

"Zee tunnel, zee cavern—it'z all caving in!" He grabbed KC and Bear, quickly pushing them forward. "Run!" he shouted. "Run vor your livez!"

Melissa looked back at the hole. The old man was right. What had been a two-foot wide opening was now six feet . . . make that ten . . . make that it was getting bigger by the second!

Quickly, she stooped down to Spalding, slipping her

shoulder under his arm, trying to get him to his feet. "Sean," she shouted, "give me a hand. We've got to get Spalding out of here."

Sean joined her, grabbing Spalding's other arm. And just in time. Suddenly the ground where Spalding had been lying gave way, splashing into the cavern below.

Melissa screamed. But it wasn't over. Not by a long shot.

A chunk of ground crumbled directly under her foot and fell away. She ran forward, dragging Spalding with her. "We've gotta get outta here!" she shouted. She turned to Spalding. "We've got to get you to solid ground!"

"But . . . the treasure . . ." Spalding protested.

"Forget the treasure!" Sean shouted from the other side. "Just move your feet! We've gotta get out of here!"

Directly in front of them, a huge piece of rocky shore fell away. It was at least twenty feet long and almost that wide as it crashed into the water with a thundering roar. "The other way!" Sean yelled. "We've got to go the other way!"

Melissa nodded and headed in the opposite direction, up the steep cliff. But suddenly the cliff itself began to shake. They leaped back just as tons of rock and dirt gave way, falling into the cavern below.

Melissa screamed.

Now they were cut off in the front and the back.

"Over there!" Sean pointed. "Over to the right."

They veered to the right, still dragging Spalding with them. The ground shook so hard that they could barely stand. The air continued to thunder with crashing land and roaring water. Off in the distance, Melissa heard the others shouting and Slobs barking, but she was concentrating so hard on trying to stand that she paid little attention.

"LOOK OUT!" Sean cried as another crack appeared in front of them, then slipped into the churning water.

Melissa spun around, desperately searching. They were cut off! They stood on a small island of land less than ten feet wide. Everything else had fallen away.

Well, almost everything.

"There!" Melissa pointed. It was a tiny strip of land jutting out from them toward the newly formed cliff. It was about thirty feet long but no more than two, maybe three, feet wide. The water splashed and frothed on both sides, but the strip seemed to be holding. At least for now.

"Are you guys crazy?" Spalding yelled.

"Do you see any other way?" Melissa shouted.

"No, but—"

"Let's go," Sean ordered, "while we still can!"

By now Spalding was able to stand on his own. As they approached the narrow peninsula of land, the rest of the group moved to the other end, shouting and encouraging them forward.

"Hurry!" the old man called. "It'z going to cave in. Hurry!"

Sean turned to Melissa. "I'll go first!"

She started to protest.

"If it gives way, you can race back," he interrupted.

"But—"

Before she could argue with him, he started. She watched nervously as he inched his way across the narrow bridge of land. On both sides small amounts of dirt and rock continued to give way and fall into the raging water below, but for the most part it held.

Sean took a half-dozen steps before motioning them to follow. Spalding went next. Melissa gave him several feet leadway before she also stepped onto the tiny strip of land.

She was terrified, big time. The water kept splashing and roaring on both sides as the little land bridge kept eroding and growing more and more narrow. Melissa told herself there was nothing to fear, that it was no different than walking the neighbor's fence. (Although the neighbor's fence was only five feet high with a nice soft lawn to fall on, as opposed to a fifty-foot dropoff onto sharp rocks and swirling water. Other than that, they were exactly the same.)

"Don't look down!" Sean yelled. "Just keep looking up at the others."

Melissa obeyed, keeping her eyes straight ahead. Slowly, the three made their way across the narrow peninsula, step by step, foot by foot.

At last Sean reached the cliff and was pulled onto the solid ground by the others.

Next it was Spalding's turn.

Now there was only Melissa. She had less than a dozen feet to go. Just a dozen short feet and . . .

Suddenly something caught her eye. Off to the right and down in the water.

It was the treasure chest. Floating. It was slapped to and fro by the water, but it was definitely floating.

"Don't look down!" Sean shouted. "Don't look down."

But it was too late. The height, the crashing water, the

deadly rocks—they all took their toll. Suddenly Melissa was feeling very light-headed.

"Misty!"

She slowed to a stop, barely able to keep her balance, afraid to move.

"Don't look down!" Sean cried.

But Melissa couldn't help herself. She couldn't take her eyes off the chest and the water and the rocks. She closed her eyes, trying to get her bearings. But when she reopened them, the chest was still there, along with everything else.

"Look at me!" Sean shouted. "Misty, look at *me*!"

She threw him a brief glance before looking back down again. More and more earth gave way beside her feet, but she couldn't move. "Help . . . me . . ." she cried.

"Misty!" Sean shouted. "Misty, listen to me."

Again she looked up.

"It's just like Peter walking on the water," he shouted. "Remember, in the Bible? When he kept his eyes on Jesus, he could do it, remember?"

Melissa gave a half nod and looked back down. There was the chest and the water and the—

"But when he looked down," Sean continued, "when he took his eyes off Jesus and looked at the wind and water, remember how he sank?"

Melissa nodded and glanced back up at him. Sean had taken a half step toward her, back out onto the narrow strip of land.

"It's the same thing here," he shouted. "Don't look down. Don't pay attention to the water or the rocks or that treasure. Just keep your eyes up here." He stretched out his hand. "Just keep your eyes on me and start walking."

Melissa swallowed and took a tentative step toward her brother.

"That a girl."

And then another.

"You're doing fine." The others also started shouting encouragement.

But once again the temptation overwhelmed her. Once again the glittering chest caught her eye, and once again she had to look down.

"Misty, no!" Sean shouted. "Keep your eyes up here. Don't look down. It's just like Dad said: Keep your eyes on God. He's the real treasure. It's not down there—it's up here. Keep your eyes fixed up here!"

Melissa continued staring at the chest.

"Misty . . ."

And then she heard it. Felt it, really. The ground began to shake violently.

"Run!" Sean shouted. "Misty, run!"

She saw his face fill with terror. She threw a look over her shoulder and saw the reason. Directly behind her, the bridge was falling away.

"Hurry!" Sean shouted. "Hurry!"

She began walking, fighting to keep her balance amidst the shaking and rocking.

"Faster!" Sean yelled.

"I'm going as fast as I—"

"RUN!" he shouted. "MISTY, RUN!"

Now she felt the bridge giving way behind her—felt it slipping just behind her heels.

"RUN!"

She broke into a sprint, still unsteady. Maybe she'd reach her brother before she slipped, maybe she wouldn't. It didn't matter. Not now.

She was ten feet away. Then five. Three . . .

Suddenly the ground gave way under her left foot. She lost her balance. She started to fall.

"SEAN!"

She was falling backward. Tumbling, plunging into the raging waters and the crashing—

When suddenly she felt a hand grab hers. She looked up. Sean was leaning down over the cliff. Bear and the old man were holding him as he stretched out, hanging on to her hand.

Melissa didn't have the strength to hold on. But Sean did. He quickly pulled her up and onto the solid rock just as the last of the land bridge collapsed, pounding and thundering as it crashed into the sea below.

10

Wrapping Up

FRIDAY, 11:59 PDST

Everyone lay out on the rocks, catching their breath. The ground had finished falling into the sea, and the ocean had pretty much stopped all of its spraying and splashing. Now everything was growing calm and peaceful.

It was hard to imagine. Just a few minutes earlier, there had been a beautiful rocky beach in front of them. Now the beach was gone and replaced by a jagged cliff over the ocean.

"I don't get it," Sean finally said as he turned to the old man. "How did you know where to find us?"

The old-timer shrugged. "Ven I come back vor more

ztuff, I zaw zee hole in zee church vloor. It vaz zhen I knew you had gone avter zee treazure."

"And you knew we'd get stuck in that shaft?" Melissa asked.

"I knew it vould be high tide, and I knew you vould ztop at nozing until you vound my treazure."

"*Your* treasure?" Spalding challenged.

"Of courze." He looked sadly out onto the water where the chest had last been seen. "In zat chezt vehre all me clothez I'd been ztoring."

"Clothes?" little KC croaked. "You mean, there were only clothes in that chest?"

"Of courze . . . clothez and me bookz."

"Books?" Melissa asked in surprise.

The old man nodded. "Zey are me treazure, all zat I own." He sighed sadly as he continued to look out over the ocean. "And now zay are gone . . . zay are all gone. . . ."

"We risked our lives for a bunch of old clothes and some books?" Sean repeated in amazement.

The old-timer looked at him and nodded.

"But that chest," Spalding interrupted. "It was solid gold."

The old man shook his head. "It vas painted vood."

"Wood?" Spalding cried.

"I am avraid zo."

"But what about all those jewels on top?"

"Jez colored glazz I glued on."

Spalding let out a loud groan.

"Wait a minute," Melissa said. "What about ZEEG REEED? If those were just clothes and old books, why was this monster protecting it and trying to kill us?"

"Monzter?" the old man asked, frowning. "Zere vas no monzter."

"Of course there was," Sean argued. "He chased us through the tunnel. In fact, he nearly caught us a couple times."

"And you warned us about him," KC added. "You kept saying it would eat us up, that it would destroy us."

"And zo it nearly did," the old man nodded.

"But you just said it doesn't exist!" Sean exclaimed.

"I zaid it iz not a monzter."

"What is it, then?" Sean asked. "Where did it come from?"

"Vhy, it comez vrom your heartz, of courze."

"Our hearts?" Melissa asked.

The old-timer nodded. "Of courze. GREEED hidez in all our heartz. It—"

"Wait a minute," Sean interrupted, "did you say 'greed'?"

"Yez. ZEEG REEED—it iz a terrible zing zat livez inzide each—"

"ZEEG REEED?" Spalding repeated. "I don't understand."

But Melissa did. "Hold it a minute. Maybe he doesn't mean 'ZEEG REEED. . . .' "

The others looked at her, waiting for more.

She continued. "I think he might mean 'ZEE GREEED.' " She began to nod. "Of course it's not 'ZEEG REEED'—it's 'ZEE GREEED.' That's what he's been saying. 'Beware of ZEE GREEED'—*THE GREED*."

"Exactly," the old man insisted. "Bevare of ZEE GREEED. Bevare of ZEE GREEED. . . ."

Now it was Sean's turn to nod. He remembered all too well the warning the old man had given them earlier. "It will eat you up," he quoted softly. "It will devour you. Beware of the greed."

"Exactly," the old-timer insisted. "Bevare of ZEEG REEED, bevare of ZEEG REEED."

Sean and Melissa shared looks. All this time they'd been running from some monster they thought had been chasing them. And all this time it was only imaginary.

Just something in their minds. It wasn't anything harmful or dangerous.

Then again, maybe it was. Maybe it was more dangerous than they knew. After all, their greed nearly *had* devoured them. It nearly *had* killed them. Maybe ZEEG REEED was far more dangerous than any of them had imagined.

Well, any of them except Bear.

"So," Bear glanced around nervously, "do you think he got out of the tunnel before it caved in? Will he still be coming after us?"

Everyone snickered. Somehow Bear still hadn't gotten it.

Sean smiled and slapped him on the back. "I don't think we have to worry about him for a while."

A wave of relief crossed Bear's face.

"But it's important we stay on our guard," Melissa added. "If we're not careful, he can always come back."

FRIDAY, 16:29 PDST

"Okay," Sean said as he stood in front of the radio station's van. "I'll go on the air first and tell them about the tunnel and stuff, and then you can—"

"Hey, wait a minute," Melissa protested. "Why do you get to go on first?"

" 'Cause I'm the one with this cool Hawaiian shirt."

Melissa cocked her head and looked at him. "Haven't we already had this argument?"

Sean nodded. "That's right, and I won, remember?"

Melissa let out a long, low sigh as she glanced at the church below them. Because of yesterday's catastrophe, they weren't allowed anywhere near the auction. Instead, they had been stuck high atop the hill to report the news story from a safe distance away.

Down below were the mayor, Spalding's father, Mrs. Potts, and the usual crowd. Twenty-four hours had passed since the last time everyone had gathered there. And in twenty-four hours, nothing much had changed. Well, nothing except Middelton acquiring a brand-new coastline, the complete destruction of a secret underground cavern, a few hundred scratches and bruises on Sean's and Melissa's bodies, and, of course, a deeper understanding of the dangers of greed. Other than that, everything was pretty much the same.

"Okay," Herbie whispered. The station's engineer stood near the back of the van, eating a hot dog with one hand and holding a headset to his ear with the other. "You're on in 3, 2, 1 . . ."

Sean cleared his throat and began. "Good afternoon. This is Sean Hunter reporting live for radio station KRZY. In just a few moments, the leaders of our beloved city will be auctioning off this beautiful old church that you see below me."

"It's radio," Melissa whispered, "they can't see the church."

But Sean was acting too much like a hotshot to be bothered by details. He continued. "A church that has been part of this city's heritage for hundreds, perhaps even *thousands*, of years."

Melissa rolled her eyes so hard she practically sprained them. The city was less than two hundred years old. How could the church have been there for thousands?

" 'And why?' you're asking yourself. Well, I'll tell you why. So they can tear it down and build a parking lot for a new bank. And if you ask me, which you haven't, but I'll tell you anyway. . ."

It was about this time that Melissa knew she'd never get the microphone. Sean was on a roll and would be hogging the glory for the rest of the newscast.

He continued. "The reason is greed. That's right—plain, simple greed." He stuck his hand into his pocket and continued more casually. "Now, this particular reporter has had vast experience with greed, and I'll be happy to share with you some of my incredible insights. . . ."

Melissa blew the hair out of her eyes. Her brother may have had experience with greed, but he had a lot to learn about humility. She watched as he casually leaned against the van. Normally, this wouldn't have been a problem—except that the van was parked up on the hill. Even that wouldn't have been so bad if Herbie had remembered to set the emergency brake.

But, of course, he hadn't. So Sean's extra weight gave it all the excuse it needed.

The van started moving. Sean jumped back. He desperately motioned to Melissa to do something. She did. She desperately motioned to Herbie to do something. Unfortunately, ole Herb was too busy keeping Slobs away from his hot dog to see or do anything.

So the van continued its merry way, quickly picking up speed as Sean and Melissa stood, staring at it in amazement.

But they weren't the only ones to see it. Eventually

Mrs. Potts glanced up from the crowd and saw the van rolling directly toward them. Immediately she did what she did best. Immediately she put into practice that little something she'd learned since becoming neighbors with Sean and Melissa.

She screamed for her life!

Once she'd started screaming, she began the running (something else she'd picked up from the brother and sister team).

Others looked up. And realizing that it wouldn't hurt to follow her example, they, too, began screaming and running for their lives. Soon everyone, including the mayor, had joined in the fun and games.

Sean and Melissa exchanged glances. But it wasn't over—not yet.

The first to go was the lectern the mayor had been speaking from. The van crashed into it, exploding it into a thousand pieces. Next came the chairs. Same crash, same flying pieces. And last, but not least, was the newly installed fire hydrant. It flew nowhere . . . but its water shot up, spraying everywhere.

Yes sir, it was just like old times: drenched people shouting and shaking their fists, Mrs. Potts dropping to

123

her knees in sobbing hysteria, and Slobs barking and baying at all the commotion.

Sean and Melissa shook their heads in wonder. What a strange comfort it was to know that as much as some things change, other things will always remain the same. . . .

By Bill Myers

Children's Series:
Bloodhounds, Inc. — mystery/comedy
Journeys to Fayrah — fantasy/allegorical
McGee and Me! — book and video
The Incredible Worlds of Wally McDoogle — comedy

Teen Series:
Forbidden Doors

Adult Novels:
Blood of Heaven
Threshold

Nonfiction:
Christ B.C. — adult devotional
Hot Topics, Tough Questions — teen devotional

Series for Middle Graders*
From Bethany House Publishers

ADVENTURES DOWN UNDER · by Robert Elmer
When Patrick McWaid's father is unjustly sent to Australia as a prisoner in 1867, the rest of the family follows, uncovering action-packed mystery along the way.

ADVENTURES OF THE NORTHWOODS · by Lois Walfrid Johnson
Kate O'Connell and her stepbrother Anders encounter mystery and adventure in northwest Wisconsin near the turn of the century.

AN AMERICAN ADVENTURE SERIES · by Lee Roddy
Hildy Corrigan and her family must overcome danger and hardship during the Great Depression as they search for a "forever home."

BLOODHOUNDS, INC. · by Bill Myers
Hilarious, hair-raising suspense follows brother-and-sister detectives Sean and Melissa Hunter in these madcap mysteries with a message.

JOURNEYS TO FAYRAH · by Bill Myers
Join Denise, Nathan, and Josh on amazing journeys as they discover the wonders and lessons of the mystical Kingdom of Fayrah.

MANDIE BOOKS · by Lois Gladys Leppard
With over four million sold, the turn-of-the-century adventures of Mandie and her many friends will keep readers eager for more.

THE RIVERBOAT ADVENTURES · by Lois Walfrid Johnson
Libby Norstad and her friend Caleb face the challenges and risks of working with the Underground Railroad during the mid–1800s.

TRAILBLAZER BOOKS · by Dave and Neta Jackson
Follow the exciting lives of real-life Christian heroes through the eyes of child characters as they share their faith and God's love with others around the world.

THE TWELVE CANDLES CLUB · by Elaine L. Schulte
When four twelve-year-old girls set up a business doing odd jobs and baby-sitting, they find themselves in the midst of wacky adventures and hilarious surprises.

THE YOUNG UNDERGROUND · by Robert Elmer
Peter and Elise Andersen's plots to protect their friends and themselves from Nazi soldiers in World War II Denmark guarantee fast-paced action and suspenseful reads.

*(ages 8–13)